Regal
Hallowe
By Victoria

Cover art by Tabatha Füsting

To Kiley

Enjoy the stories :)

V. Bates

5th August 2023

Mokoto

'The Gods can control our dreams. If they love us, they can appear to us in dreams, and bring back lost friends and family for a happy reunion. However, they can also be cruel and bring back enemies… in nightmares.'

- Source unknown

*

It was late into the night when Prince Mokoto of the planet Gaiamiráka finally retired to bed. After a late training session and a lukewarm shower he stealthily stepped into the room of his wife, Lakuna. He could see her outline through the darkness; she was fast asleep in bed. He removed his clothes and slipped in beside her, placing a possessive arm around her smaller frame. She stirred into his warmth, but his presence wasn't enough to wake her. Not that he had wanted to wake her. What he wanted was sleep. His eyes were heavier than usual, his body much more drained than he'd been expecting… Perhaps he had caught a sickness. Mokoto sighed quietly, and allowed himself to fall into the dark clutches of sleep. As he began to drift, he started to feel cold…

*

'The Goddess of Death is always following us. If we have life left in our souls we will not see her, but if it is our time we will feel cold, and then we will see her... and when we see her, then there is nothing in the world that can save us.'

-   Source unknown

*

Mokoto awoke shivering, which wasn't like him. He was a warrior; he had been raised to endure cold, and pain, and discomfort... very rarely did the cold bother him, but it bothered him now. This was more than cold. When he opened his eyes he could feel his body shaking; his sharp teeth trembled in his mouth. He sat up in bed, snarling in anger.

"What's wrong with this place?" he hissed. "Laku, do you feel that?"

She didn't answer. How could the cold not bother her? If he couldn't even sleep through it he doubted she could. She was a warrior as well, but she wasn't as strong as him. "Laku –" he reached down, but his wife wasn't there. Mokoto paused, startled by the emptiness he felt at his side. It wasn't just his wife that had gone... Mokoto's outstretched hand passed through thin air, when it should have landed on his bed. He gasped, and looked at his hand through the darkness. Then a sharp coldness struck his heart. It wasn't fear, it was confusion... which for a warrior such as Mokoto was terrifying. This was not his bed. This was not the large, comfortable bed he had fallen asleep in. This bed was barely big enough to hold his body alone. Suddenly Mokoto could feel how hard it was; how worn and damaged was the mattress, how thin the sheets… This bed reminded him of… that place.

Mokoto closed his eyes, attempting to push himself back into reality, but it only made the memories of his childhood stronger. His childhood in the Hive. The school of the warriors. The rooms were small. There were no windows; darkness was a part of everyday life. The walls were cold and bare; the floor was hard and dirty. The smell of blood was thick in the air; the horrific sound of children screaming echoed through every hour of the day. His tutors beat him for everything he did wrong. He was starved and frightened as a child, knowing only loneliness and pain… It was a long time ago now, but Mokoto recalled it vividly. The more he recalled it, the more real it became… Then he had to realise. He was back in the Hive. "No!"

He snarled, and snapped his eyes open. He looked around the room; it was pitch black, but he knew where he was. This was his old room. His old room in the Hive! "No!" Mokoto roared into the darkness. "I graduated! I don't belong here!" He jumped off his bed and ran for his bedroom door, but it wasn't there. In his haste he assumed he had remembered it wrong; the door must be in another part of the wall. He felt his way along the cold walls of this small room; his eyes weren't adjusting to the darkness. They should be. He should be able to see, but he couldn't see a thing. Not even the worn bed. His claws scraped

5

against the walls as he searched frantically for the door. It wasn't here… He must have travelled the length of the room by now, but the door wasn't here… and the room felt smaller. Why was it smaller? "Let me out!" Mokoto boomed, slamming his clenched fists into the wall. He heard it crack under his strength; the crack echoed through his ears, loud enough that he was sure the wall would collapse… but it didn't. This wall was indestructible. Nobody could defeat the Hive.

Mokoto stepped back, and jumped. There was another wall behind him. He'd stepped back into another wall – how? He knew this room like the back of his hand; he knew how big it was. But it was smaller… Where was his bed? Mokoto clumsily felt his way through the darkness, and he stumbled onto it. The tired frame creaked as he crawled over it, and he sat upon the worn sheets. He threw his hand out to the side of him, and cried out when his knuckles crashed into the wall with a harsh *crack*, followed by pain. No… no, this was impossible. Frantically, he threw his other hand out, and felt pain again. The walls were at either side of him; the room was the width of the bed. How? It made no sense. What was he doing here? "Father!" Mokoto screamed into the darkness, his eyes wide. His heart was racing; he could hear his own frantic heartbeat loud in his ears. His setules were raised, his Gaiamirákan body panicked. He hadn't felt like this since he was a child… he was frightened. "Father!" He called a name he had never called as a child. As a child he knew his father wouldn't save him; his father wasn't in the Hive. His father, the king of Gaiamiráka, was in the palace. The palace where Mokoto had been sent to live years ago, when he had become good enough to leave the Hive. The palace where Mokoto had fallen asleep... The palace where Mokoto now lived with his father, because he'd earned his right to be there! He shouldn't be here! "Father!" He screamed at the top of his lungs, his fear never ceasing to grow. He couldn't think. It never occurred to him that his father wasn't here. It never occurred to him that nobody could save him now. In the Hive, nobody could be saved. In the Hive, you were alone. "Father –"

Mokoto stopped, as did his heart. Why hadn't he heard that...? He was sure he'd called out into the darkness, but he'd heard no sound escape his lips. "F-Father...?" Mokoto breathed into the endless black. Nothing... He wasn't making a sound. He tried to scream again, and again, but nothing. Nobody could hear him... and it wasn't his own hearing that had failed. Mokoto could still hear everything else... He could hear screams. The screams of his peers, being beaten and tortured. The sound of broken bones and blood; the sound of anger as tutors punished their students. Then breathing...

Mokoto's wide eyes moved around in his skull, trying to see... but they could see nothing. Mokoto could say nothing. But he could hear. He could hear the sound of breathing. It wasn't coming from one direction; it wasn't a person in the room with him. It was the walls... it was the Hive. The Hive had him... and it didn't want to let him go. "No!" Mokoto tried to scream, but once again he couldn't. All he could do was hear the breathing, and the heavy beating of his own frightened heart. He could feel the trembling in his body as it became colder; it was a wonder he was still alive. The Hive wanted him alive. "Fa – ugh!" Mokoto gagged as a sharp, heavy pain coursed through his stomach as if he had just been punched. He could taste blood in his mouth; he could smell it on his clothing. He really was back here… "No! No! I don't belong here!" Mokoto tried to shout, but still he wasn't making a sound. He held his arms up in defence, but it made no difference. The coldness still surrounded him; the breathing became loud enough to drown out his own heartbeat. He felt a pain in his jaw, and the taste of blood became stronger. He felt a tug in his shoulder, followed by more pain. The Hive had him… "No!" Mokoto snarled, and he suddenly felt different. All of a sudden his fear turned into anger, and he jumped up on his bed. "I don't belong here!" He roared, and he flung his foot into the wall. It hurt, but he didn't care. He did it again, and again. As if he could kill this place. "Let me out!"

Gasp! In the middle of the night, the sleeping Prince Mokoto sat up in bed. He was panting heavily, his eyes wide and his setules raised. Sweat poured down his back and onto the large, clean mattress below him. Then at his side, his wife started to stir.

"What's wrong…?" She mumbled sleepily.

Mokoto looked down at her. He was confused at first. Then he came to his senses… and embarrassment became the strongest emotion he had felt all night.

"Nothing." He grunted. He lay back down and closed his eyes, daring the nightmare to return.

*

'Sometimes the Gods don't send nightmares because they hate us. Sometimes… they just do it for fun.'

- Source unknown

*

"Trick." Elsewhere, in the centre of the world, in the Realm of the Gods, a mischievous goddess giggled to her companions. "What did you think of that?"

"I think if the people knew the Goddess of Love gave them nightmares, they wouldn't have much faith in love." A cold goddess spoke from her side, with a small smirk upon her lips.

"I always did like Halloween…" The Goddess of Love answered. "And he deserved it. I'm sure he'll appreciate his wife more now. It's nice to be reminded of what you have."

"Very good." The God of War spoke. "Next year, let's go after her."

"No… She already appreciates him." The Goddess of Love smiled, and she watched fondly as Mokoto and his wife slept the rest of the night in peace. "Happy Halloween…"

Anaka

'The Gods can control our dreams. If they love us, they can change our dreams, and give us everything we have ever desired. However, they can also make our biggest fear come true… in nightmares.'

- Source unknown

*

It wasn't drastically late into the evening, but the warrior Princess Anaka of Gaiamiráka was exhausted all the same. She hasn't slept in over a day, a fairly regular occurrence for her. She always got too sucked into her work, and even when she left the premises of the Royal Laboratory of Science, where she was a key member of staff, she still worked on her laptop for hours. It wasn't uncommon for her to fall asleep in front of it, and that was what she had done. She didn't even notice a holy presence surrounding her.

*

'The God of Wisdom has no time for ignorance or fools. He blesses many of us with knowledge and intelligence, and expects us to use it wisely. However, if he is displeased with the way we have used his gift, he will not hesitate to take it away.'

-   Source unknown

*

Anaka awoke with a start only a couple of hours later. She rubbed her eyes and looked up at the sound of footsteps. Then she smiled as her husband and employer, Raikun, approached her.

"You're still working on that?" He commented, moving his eyes to the laptop in front of her.

"Oh… mm." Anaka nodded. "I'm nearly done."

"Anaka…" Raikun sighed. "Don't. It's over. You'll only anger your father if you carry on."

"What do you mean?" She frowned.

"Well, he must have shut us down for a reason." Raikun took a seat beside her. "I was hoping you could find out what that reason was."

"Shut down?" Anaka looked at him, bewildered. She felt so confused… as if the world had changed while she was asleep. She had a terrible sickly feeling all of a sudden, a cold panic steadily making its way into her heart…

"Yes…" Raikun gazed back at her, with the same bewildered expression upon his face. "Your father has stopped funding the Royal. We can't raise the funds ourselves – we can keep a couple of departments open, but –"

"Wait, what?"

Anaka rubbed her head and closed her eyes. She had a headache... it wasn't like her. Normally she wasn't so easily disturbed, but... this didn't make any sense. She was so confused it was making her dizzy... "What are you talking about, Raikun?"

"Anaka – what do you mean?" Raikun frowned. "You know what happened – your father has shut the Royal down. We still have the military department, and we can afford to run about a quarter of the rest... but most of the Royal is gone – my salary has been halved. We've had to let everybody go – you don't remember that?" He watched her, and the lost expression upon his wife's face made him concerned. She didn't look herself... She was pale, and confused... How did she not remember...? "Today we were clearing out – you helped pack the equipment away, remember?" He reached out his hand, to touch her face. "Anaka –"

Raikun stopped when she flinched away. Anaka's eyes darted around her skull, trying desperately to recall memories that simply were not there. She remembered having a normal day at work, and then she had come home to finish her project... There had been no mention of shutting down, or lost funding, or... any of this. No... no! She didn't believe it. Her heart was racing; she felt nauseous. The Royal couldn't shut down! Her father would never – he knew what it meant to her! The Royal was her whole life – no, no! No she didn't believe it! Not without seeing it for herself – she had to see this for herself! Her heart still racing and her eyes wide, she jumped to her feet.

"I – I have to go!" Anaka stammered. "I have to see it!"

"Anaka –"

"I'm going!" Anaka shrieked, and bolted out of the room.

She charged down the corridors of the palace, her breaths short and frantic as she made her way outside and into a car. She screamed at the palace chauffer to take her to the Royal, and when they arrived she practically tore the car door off trying to get out. She ran into the building, up to her floor... and then she stopped. She stopped moving. For a moment, she stopped breathing. Her heart stopped beating. She was... stunned.

He was right... there was nothing here. No computers, no people... the Royal was open day and night; there should be somebody here at all hours, but... there was nobody. Anaka walked around, peering through the windowed doors of research rooms – rooms that should be full of equipment and specimens... nothing. Every room was empty. All the equipment, gone. All the projects, gone. All the research... the research she'd put her life into – she, and everyone else. Everyone that wasn't here... No. No... No no, no!

"*No!*" Anaka screamed, grabbing at her own hair to stop herself breaking down the walls. "No!" her breathing became rapid; she could hear her own panicking heart pounding in her ears. She was trembling; her eyes were stinging with the warm stickiness of tears. This couldn't be happening. This could *not* be true! Why would he do this? Why would her own father do this?

Anaka wailed, her grip on her hair tightening as her vision changed. She didn't even notice her legs collapsing, but when everything seemed lower she assumed she must have fallen to the floor. She dug her claws into its hard surface, hissing as they cracked against it. The pain was nothing. Not even a distraction. In fact it just made her despair worse, and she felt even more panicked than before. No! No no no no *no* –

"Anaka."

Anaka gasped at the sound of her father's voice behind her, and a jolt of something hot and sharp shot into her heart. She felt a terrible burning within her; an overwhelming need to harm this man... the king of Gaiamiráka. She couldn't care less about his crown now; she couldn't care less than she was his child, and that she should always respect and honour his decisions... No. Not now. She wouldn't obey him now. He was wrong! The intelligent scientist side of her knew that, and the warrior side of her wanted vengeance. But before she turned to let her anger loose upon him, Anaka blinked... and she heard his voice once again. "Anaka?"

He sounded closer... because he was. When she opened her eyes Anaka was no longer in the Royal. She was in the palace, in the chair in which she'd fallen asleep... and her father, King Taka, was standing over her with a drink in his hand. He looked somewhat amused.

"A nightmare?" He teased.

"... Mm." Anaka grunted, slowly coming to her senses. A nightmare...? Was that what it was...? ... What a horrible thing to experience. Why would the Gods do that to her? But, then again...

14

Anaka sighed, and shook away her discomfort. "Yes, Sire." She answered, and smiled. King Taka sniggered, and handed her his glass – the glass he had filled for himself.

"That's the downside of sleep." He spoke as he made his way to his drinks cabinet, to pour another beverage for himself. "What happened?"

"… You closed down the Royal." Anaka answered sheepishly, her embarrassment growing as King Taka started to laugh. He knew how ridiculous such a notion was.

"And you believed it?" Taka smirked, looking at her. "I would never take the Royal away from you, Princess." He took a sip of his drink. "I wouldn't dare."

He started to laugh again, and Princess Anaka joined him. He was right… King Taka was fearful of the Gods, but there were very few mortals who could control him. Anaka had always been one to get her own way.

*

'Sometimes the Gods don't send nightmares because they hate us. Sometimes… they just do it for fun.'

- Source unknown

*

"What a fool!" In the centre of the world, in the Realm of the Gods, the God of Wisdom was laughing at the princess. He had blessed many of his people with great knowledge and wisdom – enough to work in the Royal... but sometimes, through ludicrous nightmares, he did enjoy making them feel like fools.

Thoit

'The Gods can control our dreams. If they love us, they can give us wonderful dreams. ... But usually they don't.'

- Malatsa Thoit

*

Malatsa Thoit, leader of the continent Hu Keizuaka, enjoyed spending his time in the wild. His palace gardens were a mere forest, full of dangerous and exotic creatures, all of whom Malatsa Thoit had tamed. In the depths of his wilderness, amongst trees and nature, he felt most at peace. His young son Nomizon was sleeping at his side, while Thoit blew the smoke of his cigarette into the humid air. He stubbed it out on his arm and closed his eyes, relaxing enough to fall asleep himself.

*

'The Gods of Birth is a nice being. Of course he's nice, he brings life into the world... But if he wants to, he can take it away, just to see how much you miss it. So I suppose he's a maniac as well.'

- Malatsa Thoit

*

When Thoit awoke, it was to a disaster. The smell of fire pulled him from his rest, and he opened his eyes to see that his beloved forest had burned to the ground. There was smoke all around him, amidst the sound of wilting leaves and frightened animals running for their lives. Thoit's immediate thought was his cigarette, and a cold dread shot through his heart as he began to think that perhaps he hadn't put it out. Had he done this...?

His mind was in a fuzzy haze, but he was alert enough to look down. Where was his child?

"Nomi?" Thoit called into the burnt remnants of the forest. "Nomizon?" He stood and made his way through the debris, his eyes almost glistening as he looked at what had become of his creatures. There were bodies scattered all around the earth, of the animals that had been too slow or too lost in the smoke to run to safety. Thoit was a warrior, but he was not ashamed to cry... and he almost did. He almost cried at the sight of his lost animals, at his missing son and the fear he felt in his heart... when it occurred to him just how horrific this was. This was like a nightmare... and he was certain he'd stubbed his cigarette out on his arm.

Thoit stopped in his tracks, and sighed. "Alright." He grunted. "Stop taking the fucking piss." He reached into his pocket, for his cigarettes. He knew he had at least two... but his packet of cigarettes wasn't here. Much to his annoyance. Irritated, Thoit glared at the ground, towards the Realm of the

Gods. "Come on. Don't be cunts. If you are going to give me a nightmare, at least let me fucking smoke."

"That isn't a very nice way to speak to your Gods." A sweet, young female voice came from behind him. Thoit turned around to see the Goddess of Love standing there, smiling at him mischievously, her bright red eyes sparkling.

"It isn't a very nice way to speak to anyone." Thoit replied. "I want my cigarettes, then my son... and then I want to wake up. In that order."

The Goddess of Love giggled.

"Smoking is bad for you."

"So is living." Thoit shrugged.

He watched as the smoke from a burning branch beside her began to rise, and form into the shape of a female. She wore a blue dress, and blue mist surrounded her. The air turned cold suddenly... it was obvious who this was. It was the Goddess of Death, and of course she had come to say her piece.

"If you would like to die, we can make you die." She spoke. "I'm sure the God of War would enjoy killing you for speaking to us in such a manner."

Thoit stared her down, not the least bit intimidated by her. He wasn't afraid of death, not even when he was looking right into her eyes. Fear of death only tended to plague people who never wanted an end to their life. Thoit wasn't one of those people. He barely recalled when he had been. So... Thoit held the Goddess of Death's gaze, for as long as it took... and

19

eventually she sighed, and handed him a cigarette. She was even good enough to light it for him.

"Thank you." Thoit nodded, taking a drag. He allowed the smoke to settle into his mouth for a while, before he exhaled. "And tell him. Let him kill me if he wants – but then he will have to deal with me in your realm. So, it will be he who suffers." He took a drag of his cigarette again, allowing the smoke to spill from his lips as he spoke. "I'm fucking shit company."

The Goddess of Love giggled in amusement, while the Goddess of Death tried to stop a smirk forming upon her lips. "Where is my son?" Thoit demanded.

"Look around." The Goddess of Death shrugged. "What do you think happened to him? This is a nightmare."

"So not real, then." Thoit walked back through the forest, back to the spot in which he'd awoken... and he sat back down. The Goddesses followed him, and he looked up at them in spite, angry at them for giving him such a nightmare... As if his real life wasn't nightmare enough. If nothing else he was annoyed at them for taking his cigarettes away. He took another drag of his cigarette, and he exhaled as he gazed at them... and he sighed. "Can I wake up now?"

"Aren't you enjoying our company?" The Goddess of Love teased.

"Not at all." Thoit answered. "Forgive me, ladies... but I fucking hate seeing any of you." He moved his eyes to the Goddess of Death. "Except you, my dear. I'm very much looking forward to seeing you… when your so called God of War decides to end me."

"I'll bear that in mind." The Goddess of Death smirked.

"Now… if you'll excuse me." Thoit stubbed his cigarette out on his arm. "Fuck off and let me wake up – and next Halloween, please give your nightmares to someone else. My life is enough of a nightmare when I'm awake, I don't need it when I'm fucking asleep."

"You don't like seeing your animals harmed, do you?" The Goddess of Love smiled. "Or your forest?"

"No." Thoit answered.

"I'll tell the God of Birth."

"You do that." Thoit closed his eyes. "If this was his idea, tell him he's a cunt."

He was answered by the sound of giggling, and when Thoit opened his eyes he was back in his forest. In the beautiful wilderness, exotic and unharmed. The sound of birds and insects surrounded him; he could hear the soft rustling of healthy green leaves blowing in the smokeless wind. He looked down to see his son still asleep at his side, and Thoit ran a hand through the boy's hair. Thoit never told a lie; his life really was a nightmare to him… but in moments like this, at least he was granted peace.

*

'Sometimes the Gods don't send nightmares because they hate us. Sometimes… they just do it because they're cunts.'

21

- Malatsa Thoit

Taka

'The Gods can control our dreams. If they love us, they can award us with great praise and honour in dreams. However, they can also challenge us and test us… in nightmares.'

- Source unknown

*

It was late at night when King Taka, the king of Gaiamiráka, settled down to sleep. He wrapped his arms around his favourite wife, Suela, after letting himself into her room and into her bed. She knew he was there; she was a warrior, just like him, and even in her sleep she'd heard the sound of the bedroom door. She greeted him with a sleepy grunt, somewhat pleased that he had chosen to come to her room tonight. Taka had eight wives, and although Suela was the favourite, another was pregnant now. Teima. Taka sometimes spent the night in her room… out of moral obligation, Suela was sure. If Teima wasn't pregnant she would barely see him. Even now that she was pregnant it didn't stop him coming to rest with his favourite mate. He felt more at ease with Suela, and beside her he always got a more peaceful sleep… Most of the time, anyway.

*

'The God of War honours every warrior with his blood, and he expects them to honour his blood. He will slay his enemies without fear or weakness, and he expects his children to do the same. If they hold fear or weakness in their hearts then they are not worthy of his blood, and they themselves will be slayed.'

- Source unknown

*

Taka awoke to the sound of footsteps. Loud, heavy footsteps. The room was shaking… Taka sat up in bed, convinced there was an earthquake. He heard nothing, though. No rumbling, no rattling… Nothing except the footsteps. They were coming from outside.

"What's going on?" Suela's voice came from beside him, as she sat up herself. She looked towards the bedroom door, as the footsteps grew louder. The room shook with each one, their deep, thundering sound echoing off the walls.

"… Stay here." Taka said.

"Oh – shut up!" Suela frowned, glaring at him as he prepared to leave the bed. "I'm not weak – whatever's going on I can deal with it just as well as you."

"I know." Taka answered. He wasn't in fear of her life. Suela was strong, and he didn't believe he was any more capable of fighting danger than she… but there was something he felt. He wasn't quite sure what it was. An atmosphere, a sense…

24

Something told him that these footsteps were meant for him. It would be wrong for Suela to be involved. "Just stay here." He glanced at her. "If I need your help I'll call you."

"Forget it." Suela lay back down in bed and pulled the covers over herself. "You're on your own now, Sire."

"Hm." Taka smirked, and bravely made his way outside.

The corridor was dark, and empty. Everyone was in bed; nobody had come out to investigate the footsteps. The palace guards hadn't even been disturbed. It was as if nobody could hear them except Taka. They weren't meant for anyone except Taka...

He looked down the corridor, towards the sound. The footsteps were becoming louder, moving closer... Taka stared into the darkness of the corridor, his eyes searching for their source. He saw nothing. He tensed slightly, disturbed by the atmosphere. He could sense something fierce here. Something cold, and unnatural... This was the God of War. Taka knew it in his heart. He had never encountered a God before, but he knew what this was. This presence... it was not mortal. What did it want with him...?

Thud. Thud. Thud. The footsteps grew louder, so loud Taka was sure they were right in front of him, but still he saw nobody. Though he could feel them. The atmosphere grew stronger; the unnatural, immortal presence became sharp and terrifying. He felt it surround him; he felt the dark air of the corridor prickling his skin as if it had come to life. He felt a heat, in front of him... He heard the sound of breathing. The footsteps had stopped, but deep, steady breaths took their place. Taka stood his ground, although he was afraid. He was a warrior, and in the warrior clan weakness was forbidden. If he showed weakness, if he showed fear... the God of War would kill him now.

He remained perfectly still, staring into the darkness before him. He didn't dare blink. He didn't move. He could feel his heart racing in his chest; he could feel the tension of his own body... but he didn't move. He didn't back down. If the God of War was really standing before him, King Taka was staring right into his eyes... and nothing in the world of mortals would make him back down.

Then, there was silence. No footsteps, no breathing... but Taka could still feel him. The God of War was still there. Judging him. Still, Taka held his ground, and continued to stare in front of him, proving he was not afraid. He would stare for as long as it took. A long time passed, or so it felt. Then the breathing returned, as did the footsteps... and Taka heard both at his side.

He relaxed slightly. He felt the atmosphere soften around him, he heard the footsteps move past him. Had he succeeded? Had this been a test by the God of War, and had he passed? Taka didn't dare wonder too much, in case the test was not yet over. As it turned out, he was right.

He heard the footsteps stop behind him, and he heard the breathing. Then... the sound of a drawn sword. What was happening...?

"Turn." A voice spoke. Not out loud, but in Taka's mind. It wasn't his own voice. It was much deeper. Much fiercer. It was unnatural... and somehow, it was laced with blood. Taka could smell pain and war in the words, as if they were objects laid out before him. He could taste blood in his mouth – not his own. It belonged to... whoever he could smell in the words.

Taka felt afraid. He feared nothing mortal, but he feared the Gods. He feared how the God of War would test him, and what would happen to him if he failed. He had no heir – he had children of age, but none of whom he want for his heir. His heirs were his warrior children, and they were still too young to rule. There was nobody who could take his throne... and that terrified Taka most of all. He was so afraid of how much he could not afford to fail. He could *not* fail. Slowly, he took a breath. Slowly, he exhaled. Slowly... he turned around.

King Taka flinched. Not in fear, but in shock. The view he saw before him was not what he had expected. It was not his palace. He wasn't in the corridor anymore. He was... he didn't know where. There was nothing here. Nothing but an endless violet mist. Violet, the colour of the God of War. This was him. The atmosphere was stronger than ever, so strong it burned Taka's eyes. He squinted through the pain, but his eyes were open enough. Enough to see the outline of a figure through the mist. It was tall... a male. He was wearing armour, and carrying a sword... Fuck.

Taka instinctively readied himself for battle, as the figure came charging towards him. Taka was unarmed, and still in his bed clothes. His chest was exposed, and one strike from the sword would slice it in two. One strike from the God of War's sword was an instant kill.

Taka threw up his arm to catch the blade's side as its wielder lunged it at him; the sword looked slender, but pushing it aside almost broke Taka's arm. He cried out in pain, as his flesh bruised and throbbed as if it had just struck concrete. He barely had chance to feel the pain before he moved again, to evade another attack. The armoured being tried to punch him, but Taka blocked his strike. Again, the blow against his bones was heavier than it should have been; a sickening *crack* echoed through Taka's ears as his forearm was fractured. Still, Taka pressed on. He couldn't strike back; the being was too heavy and his movements too fast, too fast for any mortal to counter. Even if he could strike him it wouldn't make a difference. If this was the God of War, he could not be harmed. The God of War was invincible against mortals. All Taka could do was evade, and defend… at the cost of his own bones.

He sacrificed his arms to protect himself; he blocked every one of the being's attacks and he pushed aside the being's sword, and each time he heard his bones crack. Taka didn't run. His body was flooded with pain, but he didn't try to escape though he was sure he could not defeat this being. No mortal could defeat the God of War.

When his arms were so damaged he could no longer move them, Taka used his legs. He ducked and dived, kicking away his opponent's attacks and kicking the point of the sword away from his flesh – if it struck him even softly he would die. He leaned on his broken arms; he used them to push himself up and out of the way. Still, he never ran. Even when his legs began to break from blocking his attacker's strikes, he never ran. He knew that to run was to fail. He knew that he could not fail.

Eventually, though… it seemed he didn't have a choice. Taka was exhausted, much more than he would normally be. It was as if this being before him was draining his life, just by being near him. He felt so weak, so faint. He was certain he would die. His vision became fuzzy, trying so hard to fade. Taka wouldn't let it. As much as it pained him, he fought against the black that wanted to dominate his eyes. He struggled to see the armour-clad figure approaching him, wielding his sword. The figure was unharmed. Completely. He wasn't even slightly fatigued. He was invincible… That was all Taka could think. The figure was invincible, and Taka almost dead. Taka was on the ground. His legs had given way, but he was sitting. His body wanted to lie down and die, and he felt so weary that he almost did… but Taka fought it. He couldn't stand, but he forced himself to sit. He forced his eyes to see, through the stinging, and through the heavy headache in his skull and the ringing in his ears. He forced himself to face the God of War.

The figure stood above him, holding his sword to Taka. Taka couldn't escape. He had no means to defend himself anymore. If God of War wanted to slay him, he could easily be slayed… but he would not surrender to it. Taka stared into the figure's eyes, refusing to look away. Refusing to close them or collapse. He stared, knowing his eyes were the only weapon he had left. He knew how terrifying his gaze could be.

Taka waited for the figure to slay him. He expected to be killed, but... the figure didn't move. He just gazed back... and as he did so, the atmosphere around him changed. It became softer... but not weaker. Taka could still feel the strength of this being, as harshly as he could before. But... it was softer. Warmer. Not quite as fierce... Taka felt less of a reason to feel afraid. His fear began to subside, replaced by... something Taka wasn't overly familiar with. It was a fondness, somewhat. He couldn't describe it, nor could he explain or understand it. He felt a fondness for this being, suddenly. He felt safe around him; he felt close... He felt as if they were the same... Then Taka noticed his eyes. This being had his eyes. But it wasn't him. Taka knew that. This wasn't him... but he had his eyes. They were younger, but they were just like his. This being looked like him...

"... Taka?" Taka spoke, not shakily although he should have been afraid. He wasn't afraid. Not anymore. If this was the God of War, after whom King Taka was named, he wasn't putting fear into Taka's heart anymore. So Taka felt brave enough to speak to him, and to question who he was. Was this really Taka, the God of War?

The figure didn't respond. He simply smiled, and he put away his sword. Then, Taka felt a tiredness overcome him. No matter how much he tried, he could not fight it. He could not keep the blackness from his eyes. He felt his body lay down.

When King Taka awoke the next morning, he found himself alone. He stretched his arm out to the side; Suela was gone, but the bed was still warm where she'd lay. She hadn't left him too long ago. Had she seen the God of War as well…? … No. No, of course not. Taka came to his senses as soon as he had the thought. It had been a dream. The whole thing… a very unusual dream. He wasn't sure if there was any meaning to it, but he didn't think upon it for too long. He climbed out of bed, and got dressed, and went about his day as he usually would.

*

'Sometimes the Gods don't send nightmares because they hate us. Sometimes… they just do it for fun.'

- Source unknown

*

It was later in the afternoon when Taka found out his pregnant wife was carrying a boy. Taka immediately thought of a name. It would be Mokoto. The Gaiamirákan word for invincible.

Printed by Amazon Italia Logistica S.r.l.
Torrazza Piemonte (TO), Italy

46858450R00018